O9-BTN-556

Hunting
Grandma's
Treasures

Hunting Grandma's Treasures

by Gina Willner-Pardo
Illustrated by Walter Lyon Krudop

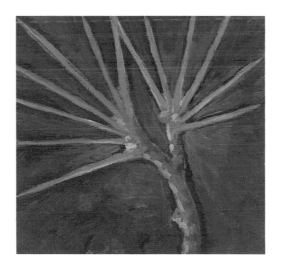

Clarion Books/*New York*

To Beth
—*G. W-P.*

To Nicole, Erik, and Matthew
—*W.L.K.*

Clarion Books
a Houghton Mifflin Company imprint
215 Park Avenue South, New York, NY 10003
Text copyright © 1996 by Gina Willner-Pardo
Illustrations copyright © 1996 by Walter Lyon Krudop

The illustrations for this book were executed in oil paint on corrugated cardboard.
The text was set in 14.5/19-point Bembo.

For information about this and other Houghton Mifflin trade and reference
books and multimedia products, visit The Bookstore at Houghton Mifflin on the
World Wide Web at (http://www.hmco.com/trade/).

Printed in Singapore

Library of Congress Cataloging-in-Publication Data

Willner-Pardo, Gina.
Hunting Grandma's treasures / by Gina Willner-Pardo ; illustrated by Walter Lyon Krudop.
p. cm.
Summary: A boy's dying grandmother helps him say good-bye and accept life's changes.
ISBN 0-395-68190-1
[1. Grandmothers—Fiction. 2. Death—Fiction. 3. Grief—Fiction.]
I. Krudop, Walter Lyon, 1966– ill. II. Title.
PZ7.W683675Hu 1996
[Fic]—dc20   94-13191
CIP
AC

TWP 10 9 8 7 6 5 4 3 2 1

Contents

CHAPTER 1

The Most Unfairest Thing

We'd had Sunday lunch with Grandma lots of times, but this time was different.

Grandma was dying.

Well, not right at the table. But she was coughing all the time now. Dad had to hold her up when she walked. She was always out of breath.

"I think it's going to be soon," I whispered.

"Shh, Kevin," Katie Rose whispered back. She pointed at our brother Ray. He was only five. "He doesn't understand. He thinks dead people just come back."

"What *I* don't understand," I said, "is why Mom and Dad are having so much fun."

"They're not. Not really," said Katie Rose. "They're pretending to have fun. So Grandma won't feel so bad about dying."

Grandma didn't like pretending. She didn't even like to play pirates. "Let's just say I'm the pirates' grandma," she'd always say.

"I don't like it," I said. "Not one bit."

After lunch, I walked Grandma to her room for her nap. We stopped at the top of the stairs for Grandma to breathe.

"Is it scary to die?" I asked. It was funny talking about dying as if it was nothing special. I felt as though I was asking Grandma to help me with my homework.

"It's scarier to be sick," Grandma said. "I've been sick a long time, Kevin."

Last summer, at Wrigley Lake, Grandma was always coughing. It was the first summer that she couldn't play shortstop or pick blackberries or water-ski.

As if she knew what I was thinking, Grandma said, "Remember last summer at the lake? At Hidden Isle?"

Every year we had a picnic at Hidden Isle. Last year Katie Rose and our cousin Lorraine got to water-ski with the grownups. I wanted to, too, only Dad said I wasn't old enough.

Grandma and I had watched the boat from the beach.

"Remember what you said?" Grandma said.

I nodded. "That this was the most unfairest thing that had ever happened to me."

Grandma smiled. A skeleton smile, I thought. "Dying's a lot like not getting to water-ski with the big kids," she said.

We started walking down the hall. Grandma leaned against my arm. She felt breakable.

I stood at the door to her room while she lowered herself into her bed. "Grandma?" I said.

She lay against her pillows, breathing. "Yes, Kevin?" she finally said.

I just stood there, crying, afraid to hear what I was going to ask.

"The thing is," I said, "how do you say goodbye?"

Grandma was quiet for a minute. "It's hard, isn't it?" she said.

I nodded. There was no sound, except for my sniffling and Grandma's rattly breathing.

Finally she whispered, "Come close, Kevin."

I moved toward her.

"I have something to tell you," she said. "Something to make saying goodbye not so hard."

That's when she gave me the envelope.

And told me the secret.

"It's easier saying goodbye when you've got someone's secret to keep," she said.

In the backseat, on the way home, Katie Rose said, "All I know is, Wrigley Lake won't be the same without Grandma."

"That's ridiculous," I said. "We can still go fishing. We can still hike out to Wrigley Falls. The twins and I can still hunt crawdads."

Delbert and Bernard and their sisters, Lorraine and Dorothy, were our cousins. Uncle Jerry and Aunt Ruth named them after dead relatives.

I rolled down the window, for air. "It won't be so different," I said.

"Grandma taught me how to catch crawdads," Dad said from the front seat. "When I was five. We'd sit on rocks in the stream. Grandma would let me wear her hat when the sun got hot."

Mom reached across the front seat and put her hand on Dad's shoulder.

"Hey! I'm five," Ray said. "Maybe Grandma will let me wear her hat this year."

"Oh, Ray," Katie Rose said, sounding tired.

"I haven't been five for forty years," Dad said, mainly to Mom, as though he'd forgotten we were there. "But today at lunch, it seemed as if I'd been five just yesterday. It was as if nothing had changed," he said sadly. "As if time had turned around."

I was used to Dad sticking straws up his nose and talking like Fred Flintstone on car trips.

Suddenly I felt mean.

"I just want everything to be over with," I said.

"Quit it, Kevin," Katie Rose said.

"I'm sick of thinking about Grandma being sick. And wondering what Wrigley Lake will be like this year." I knew I was being horrible, but I couldn't stop. "I like thinking about recess and what's in my lunch and how to spell *leopard*."

No one said anything.

"I want things to go back to the way they were," I said.

"Like last summer," Ray said. "Like the treasure hunt. Remember? Grandma hid all our clues. And at the end, I found my GI Joe. That was my favorite GI Joe," he said, "until I tried to cut his head off with the big scissors Mom says I'm not supposed to use."

Even Dad laughed. I almost told my secret right then. But I didn't. A secret was something for two people to know. Not just one. Keeping Grandma's secret, I almost felt that I was keeping Grandma alive, and that nothing would ever change.

Chapter 2
Telling My Secret

Wrigley Lake looked the same. Flat and gray, like a window or a mirror. At the south end stood Wrigley Lodge, where we ate meals and played board games on rainy days. It looked old, as if it needed paint. Just like last year.

I felt relieved. I could almost forget about the sick feeling I'd had for the last three months whenever I thought about summer at Wrigley Lake.

"See?" I whispered to Katie Rose in the backseat of the car. "It's the same. It's just like always."

"I don't know, Kevin," Katie Rose said. "Just because it looks the same doesn't mean it is the same."

"It's almost the same," I said, feeling stubborn. "We're going to go camping, and take hikes, and have a picnic on Hidden Isle, just like every year." I watched the lake slip past the car window. "I'll make it be the same," I whispered.

Katie Rose didn't say anything.

It was the first time we'd seen everybody since the funeral. Aunt Ruth pinched our cheeks and made us stand still for pictures. She had different color hair again. Uncle Jerry put his arm around my shoulders and said, "Kevin Crenshaw, I swear you're a whole head taller," which is what he said every summer.

Lorraine was wearing sunglasses, which made her look

like a grownup. She had gotten pierced ears, and a chest. Dorothy looked taller than she had last year. Dad asked Delbert and Bernard if they were still going to be scientists when they grew up, and Delbert said, "We're going to be a doctor." I thought Dad would laugh for the rest of the week.

Nobody said anything about there being only two grownups' tents this year instead of three. Or how we only had to find eleven sticks for roasting marshmallows instead of twelve.

Dinner at the lodge was fun. Dad and Uncle Jerry had a duel with their forks. Mom and Aunt Ruth pretended not to notice that we didn't eat any salad.

Still, by nighttime, we were glad to get rid of the grownups.

"Are you sure there aren't any monsters out there?" Ray asked.

I unzipped the tent and peeked out. Wrigley Lake looked black and still. The air smelled like campfire smoke and the pine trees that edged the beach. "I'm sure," I said.

"I think there are too many of us in here," Dorothy whined. Dorothy was a whiner. "Why can't the boys go back to their own tent?"

"Because," I said. "We always have a meeting the first night. To plan everything. We always do it that way."

"Last year Grandma used bug spray to keep the monsters away," Ray said.

"Shut up, Ray," I said, but I was thinking about my secret. I'd kept it for three whole months. I was almost ready to tell.

"Wrigley Lake's not the same without Grandma," Katie Rose said.

"The food at the lodge doesn't even taste the same," Delbert said.

"I think the air smells funny," said Bernard. "Not like last year."

"Grandma being dead can't change how food tastes. Or how air smells," I said.

Just then we heard footsteps. "Monsters!" Ray squeaked, but it was only Dad.

He shone his flashlight through the screen. "Ten more minutes," he said. Then we heard him heading back to the grownups' tents.

Suddenly I couldn't wait to tell. Not one more second.

"Hey, guys!" I said. "Guess what we're doing on Saturday."

"What?" Delbert and Bernard asked together.

"Having a treasure hunt!" I said.

When no one said anything, I said, "Just like last year."

"Are you nuts?" Delbert said.

Ray clapped his hands. "I knew Grandma was coming," he said.

Uh oh, I thought.

"No, Ray," I said. "Grandma's still dead. But right before—when she was sick, she told me she wanted us to have one more treasure hunt."

I pulled the crumpled envelope out of my pajama pocket. "Instructions for everyone," I said. "Just like last year."

Everyone's mouth hung open.

"No matter what we do, it's *not* like last year!" Katie Rose was almost screaming. Then she calmed down. "When did Grandma tell you?"

"At lunch," I said. "The last lunch."

"You mean you knew all this time and didn't tell?" Lorraine screeched. "*You*?"

"I did it for Grandma," I said, feeling proud.

Everyone looked impressed.

"How do you play again?" Ray asked.

"Everyone gets different instructions. They tell you where your first clue is hidden," said Delbert, showing off.

"You hunt for all your clues. The last one tells you where to find your treasure," Bernard said.

"GI Joe!" Ray yelled.

"Wait a minute," Dorothy said. "Who hid the treasures?"

"Grandma wrote the clues," I said. "But she was too sick to hide them. And the treasures. Carl helped."

Carl was the cook at Wrigley Lodge. Grandma always said Carl made the best peach pie in the whole state. Sometimes, after dinner, he rolled up his sleeves and showed us his tattoos.

Finally Katie Rose said, "It seems weird to look for something Grandma thought about and picked out just for us."

"It's like she's here," Lorraine said. "In the tent. With us."

"I want to hunt for treasure tomorrow," Ray said.

"The treasure hunt isn't until Saturday," I said. "Relax."

"Why until Saturday?" Ray asked.

"Because it's always on Saturday," I said. "The day before the picnic."

"Why?"

"BECAUSE!" we all said. Then we laughed because it was funny that we all yelled at the same time.

I waited until everyone else stopped laughing. Then I said, "Because it's how we always do it."

CHAPTER 3

Trying to Have Fun

We tried to have fun. We tried all week.

We looked for crawdads in the creek. Delbert complained the whole time.

"I told you this wouldn't be any fun," he said, plopping another crawdad into an empty coffee can.

"It's kind of fun," I said, feeling miserable.

"There were more crawdads when Grandma looked with us," Bernard said.

"I don't understand it," I said. "The crawdads don't know about Grandma. Where are they?"

There were other things I didn't understand, too. Like why the stones in the stream were sharper under my feet this year. Or why the light looked different, as if someone had forgotten to dust the sun.

I didn't say anything to Bernard. I felt crazy even noticing.

We hiked out to Wrigley Falls. Everything in the woods looked green and cool. I could hear birds, and lizards skittering across the trail, and Ray breathing hard.

"This is more like it," I said. "See? The trees don't change."

Bernard nodded. "Grandma loved trees," he said.

"Grandma would have packed us a lunch. Remember how Carl let her use the kitchen?" Delbert said. "Egg salad sandwiches with no crusts." He sighed. "I love egg salad sandwiches with no crusts."

"How much farther?" Ray asked. He looked sweaty.

"Maybe another half mile," I said. "Come on. We can swim under the falls."

"Hey," Delbert said. "How can we have the picnic at Hidden Isle without Grandma's egg salad sandwiches?"

"My dad makes great egg salad," I said. "With nuts. Quit being so negative."

Wrigley Falls looked the same. I liked the sound of the water crashing down. When the wind blew right, I tasted spray.

It was funny, though. Wrigley Falls was different without egg salad sandwiches with no crusts.

We met the girls after our hike. Katie Rose looked depressed.

"Lorraine likes boys," she said.

"What's wrong with boys?"

"I mean, she laughs a lot when they're around. She looks over my shoulder to see if they're noticing her." Katie Rose sighed. "I miss Grandma saying 'Don't be in a hurry to grow up.'" She looked at me. "Don't you miss her?"

"No," I said. "What's the point of missing someone?"

We watched some swallows dive into their nests under the rafters of Wrigley Lodge.

"Missing someone just makes you sad," I said.

"I *am* sad," Katie Rose said. "Not as sad as at the funeral. But a little bit sad all the time."

"I hate being sad," I said. "Being sad feels like being buried under sand that you can't dig out of. Like you can't breathe."

"I'm happy sometimes," Katie Rose said. "Like when I see a flower I know the name of, and remember her showing it to me." She smiled.

The swallows were making a racket in their nests.

"Every year they come back," I said. "How do they know how to do that?"

"Maybe they remember," Katie Rose said. "Maybe all winter they remember how good the worms taste and how the rafters are just wide enough for their nests."

"Their brains are the size of peas," I said. "Besides, what if all they can remember is some kid shooting pebbles at them from a slingshot?"

"I bet swallows are like people," Katie Rose said. "I bet they remember the good stuff most."

We turned to head back to the tents. Uncle Jerry waved to us from the dock. "Come for a canoe ride!" he called.

Katie Rose sighed again. "Trying to have all this fun is a lot of work," she said.

"I know what you mean," I said. I couldn't wait for Saturday.

CHAPTER 4

Hunting Treasure

Saturday finally came. Everyone ate breakfast fast.

"Who'll read my clues?" Ray whined. "Will you go with me, Kevin? Please?"

"Mom is taking you," I said. "I need to follow my own clues."

Ray ate a spoonful of oatmeal. "I already know what my treasure is," he said.

"You do not," Dorothy said, but Ray just smiled.

After breakfast, I handed out instructions.

"I think I'm almost too old to be doing this," Lorraine said, but she read her instructions and ran down to the boat dock.

Katie Rose read hers, too. "Good luck," she said.

"Same to you," I said. I unfolded my paper. For some reason, I was nervous.

It said, *Hike out to Blind Man's Rock.*

I smiled. Blind Man's Rock was on the shore of Wrigley Lake, about a half mile from the lodge. Grandma used to say it was so big that even a blind man could see it. Last summer was the first time Mom and Dad let me hike there alone.

P.S., my instructions said. *Hope you're having the best summer ever.*

I thought about how many times all week I'd wished it was last year. I was glad Grandma didn't know what I'd been thinking.

It took about fifteen minutes to get to Blind Man's Rock. It was hot. I couldn't hear birds, or lizards, or voices, or wind. Just my own breathing, and the snap of my sandals against my heels.

Blind Man's Rock was huge and white in the sun. I looked up at it and wondered where Grandma would have hidden my next clue.

Next to the rock was a bush. I squatted down. Sure enough, I saw something white peeking out from underneath.

Just for a second, I got goosebumpy, there under the hot sun. Just for a second. I could picture her knobbly fingers holding the pen. I could picture her squinting, the way she always did when she had to read her own handwriting. "Kevin, come help me make out this chicken scratch," she'd have said.

Picturing Grandma, I could feel myself starting to miss her.

I made myself stop.

Head back to the kitchen, said my clue. *Ask Carl for your next clue.*

I ran back to the lodge. I was glad my next stop was the kitchen. Hunting treasure made me hungry.

"Hey, Carl!" I called, pushing open the swinging door. The kitchen smelled like doughnut grease.

"Hey, Kevin!" Carl flipped a pancake. People staying in the lodge usually ate breakfast later than people sleeping in tents. "I've been waiting for you!"

He put down his spatula and opened a cupboard. Inside was a blue jar. Carl opened the jar and pulled out a piece of paper covered with flour.

"Your grandma said for me to keep this," he told me. "She said you'd need it."

"Thanks," I said.

"Your grandma was a very nice lady," Carl said. He unfolded some waxed paper. "Here," he said, handing me a brownie.

I took a bite. "Carl?"

"Yeah?"

"Did she . . . ? Was she . . . ?"

It was hard to ask a question when I wasn't sure I wanted to hear the answer.

"She didn't feel too bad last summer. Except for being out of breath a lot," Carl said. He picked up his spatula. "Your grandma liked thinking about all you kids looking for clues. Hunting. Remembering." He flipped another pancake. "She had a lot of fun."

It was what I wanted to know. That she'd had as good a time as we did. "Thanks," I said.

Remember Johnson's Meadow? said my clue. Johnson's Meadow was where Grandma and I flew kites.

Once we got our kite going, we would sit on a tree stump in the middle of the meadow and drink lemonade from Grandma's thermos. I knew I'd find my next clue under that tree stump.

Take the boat to Devil's Cove, it said. *Ask Dad to go with you. Wear your life jacket.*

Even while she was dead, Grandma was still worrying.

Dad was lying in the hammock pretending to read the paper.

"Sounds good," he said when I asked.

In no time, we were roaring out to Devil's Cove.

"Where will you look for your next clue?" Dad yelled over the motor.

"There's an aspen with a hole in the trunk," I said, remembering. "I'll bet Grandma put my clue in that hole."

"Grandma loved aspens," Dad said.

"Me, too," I said, but the motor was so loud that I wasn't sure he heard me.

Dad looked out across the lake. "It isn't quite the same this year, is it?" he asked.

I felt it again. That buried-in-the-sand feeling.

"Why does everyone keep saying that?" I yelled. "There's swimming and canoeing and hiking. There's hunting crawdads and camping out. There's even Grandma's treasure hunt. It's not so different."

Dad was quiet. Then he said, "Swimming's not the same without Grandma to hand you a towel. Hiking's different without Grandma to pack you a lunch."

I remembered for the first time all week that Grandma was Dad's mom.

"Turn around," I said. Suddenly I was tired. I didn't feel like treasure hunting anymore.

Dad looked at me. Then he turned off the motor. The lake got quiet. The boat bobbed up and down in its own waves.

"Grandma would like for you to keep going," he said.

"What for?" I asked. "Who needs some dumb old treasure anyway?"

"Whatever it is, I think Grandma cared about it," Dad said. "I think she'd like to know you cared enough to hunt for it."

I thought for a while. I knew Grandma would like me caring.

"Can we just sit here a minute?" I asked. I liked the quiet. I liked not trying so hard to have a good time. I liked not trying to make everything just like last year.

I took a deep breath. The air smelled piney.
Feeling sad wasn't so bad after all.
"I miss Grandma," was all Dad said.
"Me, too," I said.
This time, I knew he heard me.

CHAPTER 5

Two Kinds of Treasures

I finally found my treasure. From the aspen Dad took me back across the lake to the horseshoe pit. Then he went back to his hammock and I went to the bridge across the river. And from there to the campground, where the pine trees edged the beach.

I was the last one there. All the other kids were standing on the beach, their backs to the lake, staring at the seven new pine trees planted in the soft, red dirt.

"They were here all the time," I said, realizing. "And we never even noticed."

"Grandma loved trees," Lorraine said.

Katie Rose handed me a piece of paper. The last clue.

It said, *Treasures for every year.*

"Last year I got goggles," Delbert said. "To see underwater with."

"I got a bracelet," Lorraine said. "With a blue stone." She looked at the new trees. "It was fun getting something to wear."

I looked at her wrists. "How come you aren't wearing it?" I asked.

"The stone fell out," Lorraine said.

"Where are your goggles?" I asked Delbert.

"They're too tight this year," he said. "I guess my head grew."

"Don't you see?" I said. "Grandma gave us treasures that won't ever break or get too small. She gave us something that lasts forever."

"I still like getting things to wear," Lorraine said.

But Delbert looked up at the trees.

"I think I see," he said.

Katie Rose walked up to one of the trees. She put her face up close to its branches. "This one is mine. It smells good," she said. "All winter long, I'll remember how my tree smells."

Ray kicked up a dust cloud and stared into it.

"I thought I'd find Grandma," he whispered. "I thought Grandma would be at the end of my clues."

"Grandma's dead, Ray," I said. "She's never coming back to Wrigley Lake."

Ray nodded.

"But the trees will always be here," I said. "The trees won't change."

Ray thought for a minute. "I wish everything was like the trees," he said.

I knew just what he meant.

But the next day, at Hidden Isle, I think I changed my mind. It was after lunch. I ate so much I could barely breathe.

"Jim, this egg salad is divine," Aunt Ruth said.

"Can your stomach explode from eating too much?" Delbert asked.

I pictured Delbert's stomach popping open, spraying egg salad like confetti. I laughed.

We lay on the rocks like turtles. The sun was high and hot. I could hear waves smacking the sides of the boat, and Dorothy breathing with her mouth open.

Finally Dad said, "What we need is a little exercise." He stood up. "Come on, Kev."

"Come on where?"

But Dad just smiled.

When he pulled the water skis out of the boat, I knew.

"Me?" I asked. "Really? Me?"

"Lorraine and I did it last year," Katie Rose said. "You're just a year behind. It's your turn."

I guess I'd have figured it out if I hadn't been so busy wanting everything to be the same as last year.

"Wow!" I said, slipping my feet into the skis.

On the boat, everyone had advice.

"Hold tight," Dad said, checking the ropes.

"Bend your knees," said Katie Rose.

"Keep your arms straight," said Lorraine.

I nodded.

"Pretend you're Batman," said Ray, looking proud.

"Be careful," Mom said.

"And have fun!" Dad gave me a little push. The water felt cold and clean.

I concentrated hard. I heard the motor rev and felt the
rope tug in my hands. And then, there I was, rising up
out of Wrigley Lake, flying into the rush of the wind.

It was like getting stuck at the top of the Ferris wheel
and skydiving and hitting a home run all at the same
time. It was like how I felt on the first day of school and
the last day of school all mixed together.

It was the kind of treasure that I didn't have to hunt
for.

Flying over the waves in Wrigley Lake, I tried to think of things that would make me never forget this day and this feeling. I thought of how the water smelled as it sprayed into my face. I thought of Grandma's treasures, standing on the faraway shore. I thought about how Grandma would have clapped and cheered as I sped past the beach.

And I thought that sometimes, it was all right if things weren't the same as last year.

Gina Willner-Pardo received a bachelor's degree from Bryn Mawr College and a master's degree from the University of California at Berkeley. She has worked as an editor and now writes full time. Her previous books for Clarion are *What I'll Remember When I Am a Grownup* and *Jason and the Losers*. Ms. Willner-Pardo lives in California with her husband and their two children.

Walter Lyon Krudop received his art training at the School of Visual Arts in New York City. He has illustrated several books for children, including Gina Willner-Pardo's *What I'll Remember When I Am a Grownup*. He lives in New York City.